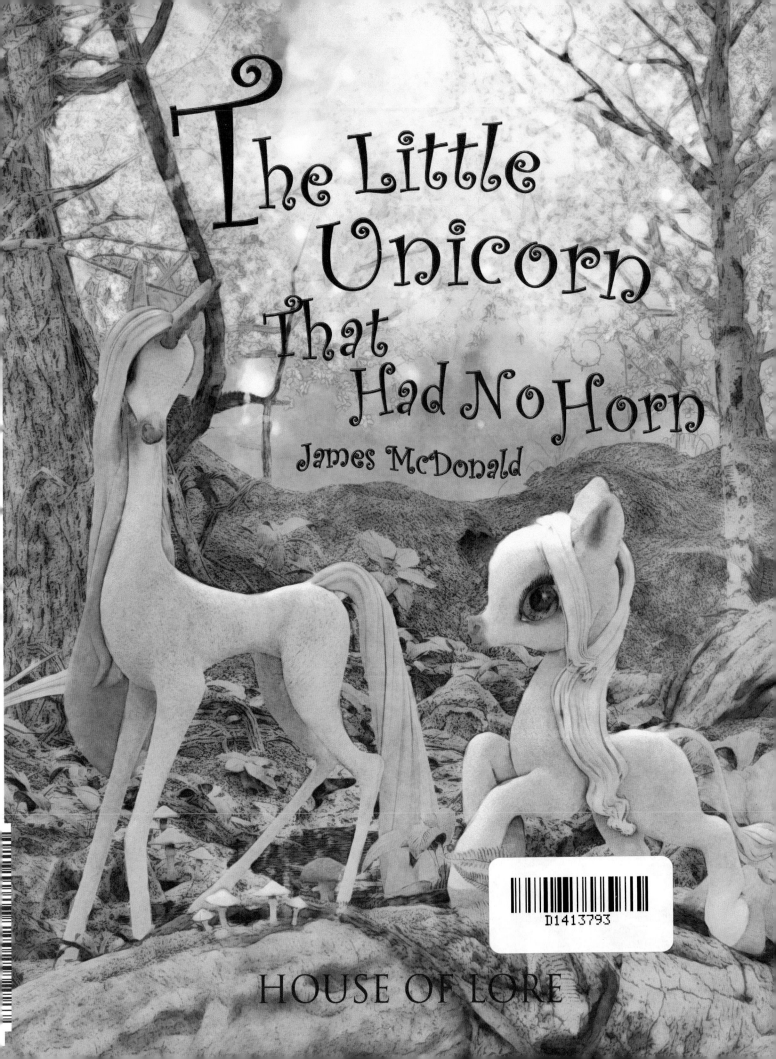

The Little Unicorn That Had No Horn

James McDonald

HOUSE OF LORE

The Little Unicorn
That Had No Horn

Copyright © 2015 by James McDonald

Requests for permission to make copies of any part of the work should be e-mailed to the following address:
Email: Business@HouseOfLore.net

ISBN: 978-0-9863151-2-1

First House of Lore paperback
edition, 2015

www.HouseOfLore.com

To my mother

On the other side of a rainbow, by the sparkling dewdrop sea, lives a beautiful mother unicorn and her sweet unicorn baby.

Ancient unicorn legends say that
when a unicorn is born, they're waiting
for that special day when on their heads
they sprout a horn.

No one has seen it happen, but we know
when the moon shines full that a horn
will begin to sprout like a vine
winding up a pole.

And so in a meadow we begin our tale of a precious little unicorn, who simply couldn't wait to grow up and receive its beautiful horn.

"Mama where is my horn? You said
this time it would come, when the
white moon rises full, chasing
away the pink setting sun."

"Be patient my sweet little babe," the mother unicorn calmly said, "it may take a bit more time for the horn to sprout on your head."

"But the full moon is forever away
and I want my horn right now!"
sulked the sad little unicorn,
with a frown and a furrowed brow.

To which the mother unicorn replied…

"I promise that you'll grow up,
so treasure each and every day.
Never wish one second of your
precious time away."

Then the little unicorn perked up
and began prancing all around until
happiness and laughter filled the air
with its friendly sound.

Pleasant days rolled right on by and
the full moon was finally here, but
the little unicorn was restless and its
heart was filled with fear.

"I'm scared my horn's not going to grow," groaned the grumpy little unicorn, "I'm scared that I may never grow and I'll never get my horn."

To which the mother unicorn replied…

"You can lay there scared and groaning about things you can never change, or you can picture in your mind running fast across the open range."

So the scared and tired unicorn
lay down its sweet little head,
and the graceful mother and child
snuggled softly down to bed.

And so too the sun went down
and the day turned into night, but
a horn was not to be for the moon
was not quite right.

"It happened once again! There's no horn upon my head. I think I'll forever sit right here and not move a hoof from my bed."

To which the mother unicorn replied…

"It's time to get up little unicorn and greet the day brave and strong, for if you never grow a horn there would still be nothing wrong."

And so the sad little unicorn tried
to do as best it could, to muster all
its unicorn strength,like a good
little unicorn should.

Many moons passed in the
sky until the leaves began to fall,
and finally the pink sun showed
its face as the unicorns stood tall.

The playful little unicorn said,
"I know this night's the one,
but even if it's not, I'll still
have lots of fun."

To which the mother unicorn replied...

"You'll always be my babe, and
I'll love you forever more. As long
as I'm alive, you'll be the one
that I adore."

So the mother and child unicorn
watched a pink sun set that day
and spoke of days gone by when
they would run around and play.

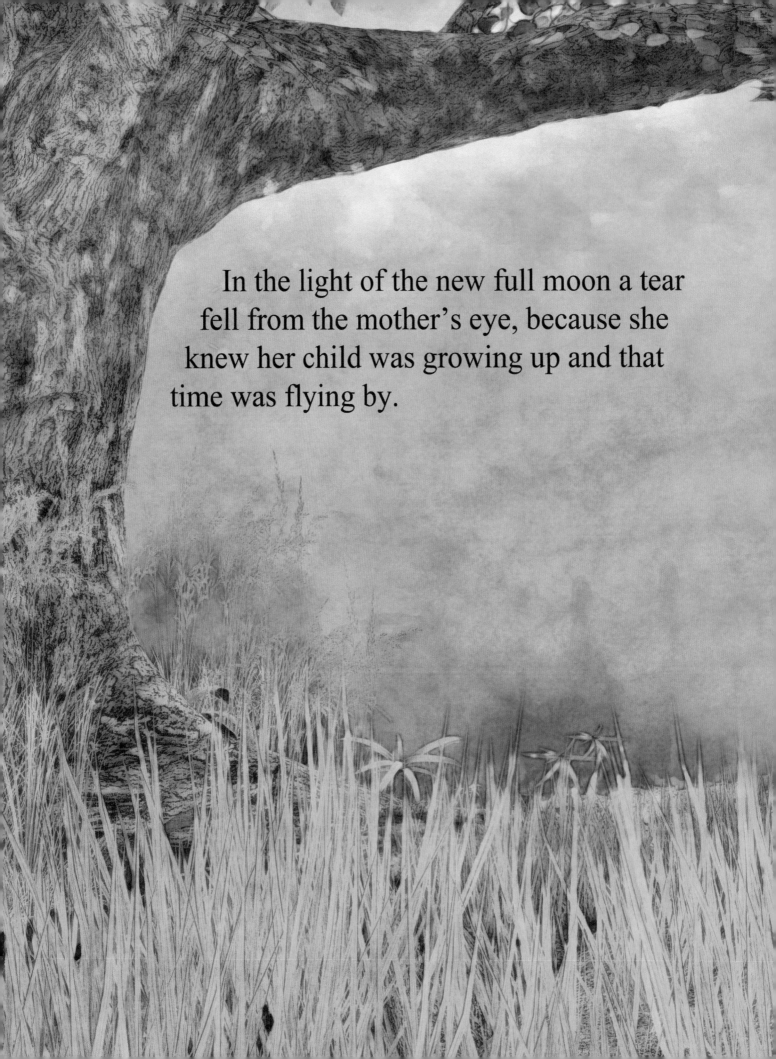

In the light of the new full moon a tear fell from the mother's eye, because she knew her child was growing up and that time was flying by.

And as the unicorn legends say, if a horn is destined to show, it will come when the moon is full as little unicorns start to grow.

Slowly under the bright moon a horn began to form, and on that night a beautiful light helped a little unicorn transform.

"Wake up my precious little one,"
the mother unicorn said, "for the
sun has awoken once more and
there's a horn upon your head!"

Then the little unicorn jumped
right up and began prancing
all about, and as the mother
unicorn smiled she sniffled
her unicorn snout.

"Now that you've finally sprouted the horn upon your head, will you use it to do harm or will you help the world instead?"

The little unicorn sat puzzled and thought
for a good long while, staring out at the
dewdrop sea until finally there
emerged a smile.

"I promise mama I'll do my best to help the world be right. I'll use my horn for good and fill darkness up with light."

To which the mother unicorn replied…

"Soon you'll grow up big and tall and
the world you'll want to see; but no matter
how you grow, or where you go...

My little unicorn you'll always be."

And so concludes the tale of the
little unicorn that wanted to grow up,
and finally sprouted a horn.

The
End